EVE BUNTING

Wanna Buy an Alien?

illustrated by TIMOTHY BUSH

Clarion Books · New York

Clarion Books
a Houghton Mifflin Company imprint
215 Park Avenue South, New York, NY 10003

Text copyright © 2000 by Eve Bunting
Illustrations copyright © 2000 by Tim Bush

The text is 15-point New Baskerville.
The illustrations are charcoal pencil on vellum.

Printed in the USA.

Library of Congress Cataloging-in-Publication Data
Bunting, Eve, 1928–
Wanna buy an alien? / Eve Bunting.
p. cm.
Summary: For his eleventh birthday Ben receives an offer of
a ride to the planet Cham with an alien named Iku, and when the appointed
meeting time arrives he is not sure if he faces an exciting opportunity
or horrible danger.
ISBN 0-395-69719-0
[1. Extraterrestrial beings—Fiction. 2. Science fiction.]
I. Title.
PZ7.B91527Wan 2000
[Fic]—dc21   98-56283
CIP
AC

BP 10 9 8 7 6 5 4 3 2 1

For Anna and Michael
—E. B.

Chapter 1

It's my birthday night and I'm sitting on my bed opening my friend Jason's present. My dog, Homer, is asleep on my pillow. He loves my pillow—I guess because it smells of me. Dogs pay you the nicest compliments. On my CD player the Beatles are singing "It's Been a Hard Day's Night."

I examine the brown paper wrapping on Jase's present. It came to my house direct, special delivery. Pretty fancy for Jase! He couldn't come to my party because he's just getting over the flu and his mom thought he needed another day at home. It's always a pain to be sick when it's school vacation, and right now we're on spring break.

Jason was bummed about missing my party and I was, too. Jase is my best friend, except for Paloma, of course. She's my best next-door-neighbor friend.

Jase's gift arrived just as we were all leaving to go see *Lost Galaxy* at the Cineplex. I hadn't had time to open the package then. Now I tear off the paper. Inside is a box, like a black shoebox, big enough to hold Reeboks for somebody who wears a size 15.

There's a bunch of stuff inside. On top is a large brown envelope and underneath it I see a tape, a paper bag, and a small white envelope. Jase has really put something together here.

I pry open the flap of the brown envelope and two photographs slide out. I stare at the one on top. Me and . . . who *is* this? The other person has his arm draped across my shoulders. We're standing on a step, but the picture is a close-up and I can't tell what kind of step it is, or where.

But the person! He's small and square and shiny silver. He's got a round head with no real nose, just two holes. His eyes are humongous and his ears are on top of his bald skull and they're big and round, too. Is it Jase? In some kind of alien suit? If so, where did he get it? And how did he fake this picture? Because he and I never . . .

I turn the picture over. On the back it says, BEN AND IKU ON CHAM, APRIL 23. The writing is not Jason's. What—and where—is Cham? And April 23? That's not even here yet. This is April 21. I know this for a fact because it's my eleventh birthday.

I put the picture down and pick up the other one, which is lying on my blue comforter. It's us again, me and Iku . . . and a spaceship. Well, obviously it's a fake model of a spaceship, a big cardboard cutout. It's the round kind like the ones they had in *Star Wars* and *Lost Galaxy*, which I saw this very day. Here are the steps again. They lead up to the spaceship and in the picture I'm climbing them, looking back over my shoulder, grinning and waving at the camera. Iku is at the top of the steps by the open hatch, which I guess is where I'm headed. There's a full moon practically hanging in a big tattered palm tree.

"This is nuts," I say out loud. "I've never even seen a spaceship."

Not that Jase and Paloma and I haven't

looked. We're all the time thinking we've spotted one, but it always turns out to be a plane or a star in the wrong place. Once it was the Goodyear blimp. We think being beamed up would be the best thing ever. Anyway, we all plan to be astronauts when we're older. We'll blast into another galaxy together.

I turn the picture over. There's no writing on this one. "Run out of things to say, huh, Jase?" I mutter.

Homer gives me the eye, bites at a flea on his rump, and burrows deeper into the pillow. "I see you're interested," I tell him.

I peer closely at the picture. Something is behind the spaceship and I recognize it. It's Ocean Lighthouse. This flying saucer, or whatever, is sitting in Ocean Field, one ck from my house. Beyond it is the tall of Surfers' Clock. It shows the time— lock.

Field is between my street and the at drop down to the ocean. I can see the amusement pier lights at night and the lighthouse beacon, too, if I don't close the slats on my blinds. Nobody owns Ocean Field. Well, I guess the city does. So there are no houses on it except the old tumbled-down wooden shelter.

People play baseball on Ocean Field and have picnics there. It's wild and windy and overgrown. Paloma and Jase and I built a tree house on the edge of the field last year, but it blew down in a huge storm. Dogs run free there. In fact, it was in Ocean Field that we found Homer one day. We saved him from the dog catcher and hid him until I could bring him home.

I reach over to stroke him and whisper, "Good dog, good Homer." He smiles at me without even opening his eyes.

For some reason my heart is flutterin These pictures with Iku are kind of s But that's stupid. This box came fro delivered by a man in a blue van. pulled a good one on me.

The Beatles are singing what Paloma calls one of their "remembering songs." "Yesterday, all my troubles seemed so far away." She gave me this new CD for my birthday. Paloma and I love the Beatles. We despise most of the hot new singing groups, but as Paloma says, "Hey—that's just us."

It's windy outside. We get a lot of wind, being so close to the ocean, a lot of fog, too. I can hear Paloma's mom's wind chimes tinkling. Those wind chimes are never quiet.

I'm listening to the Beatles and the wind chimes and I'm almost scared to look again at the box. All these other things are waiting for me. The white envelope. The bag. The tape. I'm scared and that's sappy. I hate it when I get scared for no reason.

There's a note taped to the inside of the bag, so I take that out first. It's the same writing as on the picture. But it's still not Jase's. SOUVENIRS FROM CHAM, it says. And something is very creepy about the bag. It's warm, the way it would be if it had a hamburger and fries from Slam Dunk Burgers inside. But this bag has been in the box, on my bed, in my room the whole time we were at the movies. What could be inside it?

Chapter 2

I tip up the bag. Two rocks tumble out. Each one is about the size of a grapefruit, but instead of being round, they're pyramid-shaped. And they're dark red, veined the way leaves are when you look at them closely. They lie there, red on my blue comforter, and I don't want to touch them. I'm not sure why—maybe because I've never seen rocks like this. They're the color of blood.

And those veins!

The Beatles are singing "I Want to Hold Your Hand." I need somebody to hold mine.

Homer lifts his head, yawns, and looks lazily where I'm looking. He sees the red rocks and a rumbling growl comes from his throat. The long yellow fur that ruffs his neck suddenly spikes.

I stand up. If I had a yellow ruff, it would be spiked right now, too. "What's the matter, fella?" I whisper. "What is it?"

He takes a mighty leap and starts racing

around my room, round and round, knocking over my wastebasket, his nails skidding on the wood floor.

"Wait! Wait!" I open the door and he dives through it, making these frightened little yelps.

From the kitchen I hear the slushing of the dishwasher. Mom and Dad are in the den watching the news. Everything's so normal—of course it is. Just because Jase was smart enough to find two crazy-looking rocks to freak me out doesn't mean I have to fall for it. He probably got them in one of those "Pyramids Are Power" shops or at the Sunday flea market.

I make myself walk back to the bed and pick up one of the rocks. It's warm. I peer into the bag. It's empty and it has this limpness to it, as if all the stiffening has been boiled out. I lift the other rock and hold one in each hand. Probably Jase put them in the microwave and they kept some of the heat.

I'm suddenly mad at him. A joke's a joke and I have to admit this is good stuff. Better than fake barf or rubber dog poop or one of those disgusting whoopee cushions that makes a noise when you sit on it. But he's weirding me out here. I put the rocks down and go down the hall to call him. The rest of the stuff can wait.

There's no sign of Homer in the kitchen. The empty pizza boxes from my party are still on the counter, waiting to be taken out to the trash. I lift the lid of one and there's a cold, gluey slice of pepperoni left. Normally I'd have scarfed it. But I'm not hungry.

I dial Jase's number. "How did you do all this?" I'll ask when he answers. But there's a busy signal. "Wouldn't you know it," I mutter.

Most of the time it's impossible to get through to Jase. He has a big brother, Dan, and a big sister, Daisy, and they're never off the phone. You'd think they owned the thing. "What do they talk about all the time?" I've asked Jase.

"Daffy Dan talks about girls and Crazy Daisy talks about boys. And if they're not talking about them, they're talking to them." Jase and I can't figure how he got two such doofuses in his family.

Dad comes into the kitchen. "Hi, guy!" he says. "I'm sneaking another piece of your cake. Want some?"

I shake my head. "Uh-uh."

"Everything okay?" he asks. "What did Homer do? He's hiding behind the couch."

That's where Homer goes when he's in trouble. I shrug and say, "I think something scared him."

Dad gets the cake box out of the fridge. "Hey, what did Jase give you?"

"I haven't finished opening it yet," I tell him and go back to my room.

The rocks are where I left them. The empty bag and the two photographs, too. And the box. Well, what did I expect?

I take out the white envelope. There's a letter inside on rough, dappled paper. My cousin Joan makes her own paper for cards and stuff, and this is just like it.

It's the same black writing as on the first photo. My hand is shaking as I start to read it. It says:

DEAR BEN,

WE ENJOYED YOUR VISIT TO US AND THE TALES YOU TOLD US ABOUT PLANET EARTH. WE HOPE THE EXPERIENCE WAS PLEASANT FOR YOU AND THAT YOU WILL WANT TO RETURN. YOU SEEMED TO ENJOY RESIDING WITH US.

I APOLOGIZE FOR MY EARTH LANGUAGE, BUT AS I EXPLAINED WHEN YOU WERE HERE, I AM FORTUNATE TO HAVE SOME FAMILIARITY WITH YOUR WORDS DUE TO MY FREQUENT VOYAGES TO YOUR PLANET. IF YOU WANT TO CONTACT ME TO TALK ABOUT CHAM AND ARRANGE A FURTHER VISIT, YOU WILL KNOW HOW TO DO IT. JUST GUIDE US IN. AS YOU ARE AWARE, IT WILL TAKE ONLY THREE EARTH HOURS.

YOUR FRIEND, IKU

Then there is the outline of a hand, the kind you make when you put your palm on paper and trace around the fingers. But this hand only has three fingers to go with the thumb.

I'm shivering.

Good one, Jase, I think. I like the hand routine. That's scary, all right. Okay, I give up. How did you think of all this stuff?

The date on the top is April 23—the day after tomorrow. Which means that *tomorrow* I was on Cham, or wherever. Maybe their time is ahead of ours. Like the movie *Back to the Future*—or more like *on* to the future. Getting there must be like going through a wormhole. Jase and Paloma and I'd read about those in our *Science Today* magazine. A wormhole is a tunnel through space and time with a mouth at each end. You go in one mouth and come out the other and find yourself in a whole different location in the universe. Time is supposed to flow differently inside a wormhole. You can climb through one of the mouths and go back in time. Forward, too, maybe. Scary! But nobody knows anything for sure because a wormhole in space is just a theory. Well, I for sure don't want to find out if it's true.

My head is spinning. I put my hand over the three-fingered outline. Mine is bigger. Mine is shaking!

I go to the drawer of my desk and get out the magnifying glass that came with my stamp collector kit. In the first picture Iku's arm is draped across my shoulder. Magnified, I see his hand clearly . . . yes, it's three-fingered. And creepy to the max!

Chapter 3

I try Jase again. But the line is still busy.

In our den the TV is off and Mom and Dad are playing Scrabble. They're hard-core Scrabble players.

"May Paloma come over for a while?" I ask.

Mom blinks. "Paloma?" She looks as if she's about to say, "That's not a word." Then she goes, "If her mom says it's okay. But you have to watch for her."

I nod.

Paloma and I only have to cross her yard

and my yard to visit each other, no foreign territory. We squeeze through the hedge between our houses—there's a gap about three inches wide. But our moms have a rule. After dark, we watch each other coming and going. Paloma and I think it's a sappy rule, but we're not in charge.

So I call Paloma and say: "Come on over. I have something to show you."

"Is it Jase's present?" she asks.

"Yep. But you won't believe . . . "

And then I hear her giggle.

I hold the phone at arm's length and stare at it. She knows!

"Jase told you!" I shout. "And you didn't tell me?"

"So? He's my friend, too. And he asked me to keep it a secret."

I give a disbelieving sniff.

After hanging up, I wait for her by the door. There's a full moon and I can hear the surf smashing on the rocks at the bottom of the cliff beyond Ocean Field. Full moon, big waves. The lighthouse light sweeps across our back yard, over the pen where my three turtles live, over the trees, and touches the house across the street.

"Ben!" Paloma calls. She wiggles through the hedge and slides past me, ignoring my sarcastic "Thanks a lot, pal."

We go through the kitchen to my bedroom and Paloma heads straight for the box.

"Is this it?"

"Yep. How did he do all this?" I wave my hand across the things on my bed.

"I haven't seen the results yet." Paloma picks up the pictures. I point to the three-fingered hand and she says, "Gross!"

She examines the tape, reads the letter, and touches one of the rocks. "This is warm," she says.

"I know. Are you going to tell me how Jase arranged all this or not?"

Paloma tweaks at her hair, which is something she does when she's thinking. "I dunno if I can," she says. "It's Jase's present. He'll want to tell you himself."

I grit my teeth at her. "Tell! Now!"

She sits on the edge of the bed. "Well, here's some of it. Jase saw an ad in that throw-away paper—you know, the one that always has the coupons in it?"

I nod. "Go on."

"It said, 'Wanna Buy an Alien?' and that if you're interested in outer space and want to dazzle your friends—maybe it wasn't dazzle . . . impress?—anyway, if you want to make them think you've been beamed to another planet, we can help you do it. Something like that. It sounded great."

I groan. "Oh, man!"

Paloma raises her voice and goes on. "It said they'd send all this 'proof' you'd been on another planet. Jase thought it would be terrific. He had to send pictures of you so they could fake it. And a tape of you talking—"

I interrupt. "Where did he get a tape of me talking? I hope he didn't wear a wire and record me secretly, saying stupid things. . . . And what about the rocks?"

"I don't know about the rocks. Or about the tape. How did it turn out?"

"I haven't heard it yet. Listen, Paloma." I'm embarrassed about this, but it's in my mind and I have to get it out. "This stuff is scary. It seems so real."

"It's *supposed* to be. Hey, it cost Jase forty bucks. Don't ask me where he got the money. He thinks when school starts again you can take all the stuff in and fool everyone."

"Thanks, Jase," I say, sarcastic again.

"He's bummed now that he didn't send pictures of him and me, too. We're thinking maybe we could still do that, you know. Proof that the three of us were together on Chum."

"Cham," I say.

"Wherever. Let's listen to the tape."

I'm beginning to feel pretty silly. My room is bright and warm. Homer hasn't come back, but I'm not by myself anymore and there's nothing to be scared about. Nothing. I'm beginning to appreciate my alien box. It is terrific, now that it's been explained. I'm even thinking of interesting possibilities for it.

Freddy Richter will be so mad. He thinks he's such a big shot, always getting tickets for World Series games, or going down to L.A. with his dad to see the Lakers. Nothing like that can compare, though, with what's supposed to have happened to me.

I grin at the thought and pop the tape in. Then I arrange myself comfortably, cross-legged on Homer's pillow. He may like it because it smells of me, but I like it because it smells of him.

Paloma drops into my black beanbag chair. She fishes two pieces of Bazooka gum out of her pocket and throws me one. We chew contentedly. And the tape begins.

Chapter 4

It's my voice, but different.

"I feel as though I'm the first human to set foot on this land," my taped self says.

Paloma screws up her face. "Is that you?"

"Shh!" I whisper.

A different voice. "There have been others to visit in the same way that you are visiting. I hope to favor you with an impression."

Paloma's struggling out of the beanbag chair and I'm edging off the bed.

"'Favor you with an impression,'" she says. "What does that mean? And what a creepy voice."

She's not kidding. It's dark and echoing, like a shout in a deep tunnel. I wish Homer had stayed around. He's a reassuring kind of dog.

"But soon I will have to leave." I'm talking again in that strange not-really-me way. And there's a memory attached to these words, as if I'd dreamed them once a long time ago, in another place, another galaxy, far, far away. . . . Quit it, I tell myself. This is fake, fake, fake. But my skin is creepy-crawly.

Paloma and I are staring at the tape player. The way you'd stare at a rattlesnake.

"Yes," the tunnel voice says. "You must go for now. But come back soon. I have trust that you will know how to guide us in. Perhaps, as before, you should not tell your parents. They may try to stop you. Good-bye for a little while, my friend." Then there's only the whirring of an empty tape.

There it is again. I'm supposed to know how to guide him in. If I really *had* to—I mean, if this was *fact*—I wouldn't have a clue.

I rub my arms, which are covered with goose bumps. Paloma leans against my dresser. "Man," she whispers. "That's the realest-sounding bogus tape I *ever* heard." She's tweaking at her hair again. "How did they do that?"

I rewind and we listen to the whole thing again from the beginning.

"You know what?" I say. "We've got to get hold of Jase."

I go in the kitchen for the phone. Mom and Dad are still deep in their game. "Yeah," Mom says. "I've got me a six-letter word." I look over her shoulder and see she's put down DANGER. "Coincidence," I mutter, just as Dad whoops, "How about this?" And when I look he has added an OUS. DANGER-OUS. So? It has nothing to do with me.

I carry the phone into my bedroom, and almost jump out of my bones when it rings in my hand—Iku. Calling from Cham.

It's not, of course. It's Jase.

"Did you open it yet?" he asks and he's so

excited his words jump up and down. "Is it great? I knew it would be great."

"It's great," I say.

"Did the pictures work? I had to send six for them to pick from. They kept the ones of you going up the steps into our tree house. The ones I took with my new camera."

"The tree house?" A light dawns for me. "Jase! You should see what the tree house turned into."

"I bet I know. A spaceship! Right?"

"Right." I'm trying to hold the phone away from my ear so Paloma can hear, too. "And what about the tape?" I ask. "How did you get me on that?"

"Hee, hee, hee," Jason titters. I never thought anybody said "Hee, hee, hee" except in cartoons, but Jason's saying it. "Remember when you were in the Lewis and Clark play way back in third grade?" he says. "And you were Captain Meriwether Lewis, which I still think I should have been? And you were talking to that Shoshone Indian? And my mom taped it, even though she and I were both insulted that all I got to say was, 'The horses are ready, sir'? Remember?"

"I do now." I was so relieved I almost went Hee, hee, hee myself. I'd only been eight years old then. No wonder I sounded different.

"Paloma's here," I tell Jase, and he goes, "No fair. You and she are getting to see all this first and I'm the one who paid the forty bucks."

I switch the tape on again. "Here. Have a listen."

That fake alien voice still freaks me out.

"Wow," Jason says.

I read him the letter. I ask about the rocks. He says he never sent rocks, but the ad said there would be souvenirs.

"Those guys really did a job," he adds. "I'm glad I answered the ad. We're going to fool everyone at school. And, Ben, pretend that you're going back to that planet. Pretend you've arranged to take Paloma and me with you. Okay?"

"Okay."

"I'll be over in the morning to see for myself. Mom says I should be fine by then."

"See you," I say. "Bye."

It's dark outside my window. I close the blinds. Iku could be looking in. But that's goofy. There is no Iku. Jase had just confessed.

I pick up the pictures and look again through the magnifying glass. "Two A.M.," I mutter, "and—" I stop. "Look! Take a look, Paloma. There are the two red rocks. There's one on each side of the spaceship. It's as if they're markers, guiding Iku in."

Paloma and I stare at each other.

"Are you thinking what I'm thinking?" she asks.

"The tape! 'You will know how to guide us in,' he said. Does he mean I will know how to steer him in? Tomorrow night—I mean the next morning, two A.M.—we'll bring a spaceship down to earth. If any of this is real. Which, of course, it isn't."

"Of course not," Paloma says.

Chapter 5

Y ou mean you think he's *coming?* And you think he'll take us with him . . . to visit?" Jason asks.

It's the next morning and the three of us are sprawled on the floor of my room. Jason is still sniffling a bit, even though he's supposed to be better.

"Naw," I say. "I was just doing that thing Miss Chalmers makes us do in English class. You know . . . write a story by asking 'What if?'"

Everything's cheerful and normal. The Fab Four are singing "Here, There, and

Everywhere." I can hardly believe that last night I was beginning to believe all this garbage.

"I think John Lennon was definitely the primo Beatle," Paloma says.

I shake my head. "Ringo."

"You guys!" Jase has lifted one of the rocks. "Forget the Beatles. What if Iku really is coming?"

"Give me a break," I say.

I miss Homer and I get up and call him, but he doesn't come. I think he must be out in the back yard with Mom. Sun is streaming in my window. Across the street I see Ocean Field, green, almost empty. There's just a man and a kid flying a kite and a homeless person, old Melinda May, pushing her loaded shopping cart. When I turn from the window, Jason is sniffling at the rock and then he touches it with the tip of his tongue.

"Jason!" Paloma shrieks. "That's gross! Do you want to get sick all over again?"

"I just wanted to see what it tasted like."

"You're crazy," I say. "It might be radio-active or something."

Jason drops the rock and wipes his mouth with his sleeve. "I thought you didn't believe it."

"I don't." I nod at the stuff from the black box that is scattered across my bed. "So. Tell me again exactly how you ordered all this."

"Well, first I called the 800 number that was in the ad. 1-800-AN-ALIEN.

"Let's try it now."

I get the phone and dial, but a recorded voice tells me the number has been discon-nected.

"Why don't we go over to Ocean Field and snoop around," Paloma suggests. "I mean, even if there's nothing, it'll be fun to look."

"Yeah," Jason says. "Space detectives, looking for clues. Imagine if I really did make contact. Me, Jason Liebowicz. I'll be famous."

Jason picks up his jacket, which he'd

dropped on the floor, slides his hand in the pocket, and pulls out three snails, fat in their shells. "I brought these for the turtles," he says. "I got them this morning off Mom's flower bed. There were hundreds."

Snails are my turtles' favorite treats.

We head for the back yard. I was right—Homer's out here with Mom, down where her spring vegetables are beginning to come up. The turtles, of course, are in resi-

dence. Their pen is big. Dad and I made it. The sides are chicken wire and the roof is a wire lid with a latch.

Pineapple and Coconut and Pearl wag their heads at us as we come. Like toy turtles in a souvenir shop.

We give them the snails, which they'll be munching on all day. You never saw slower eaters than turtles. Homer comes to visit and sniff around the pen. He and the turtles are pals, and after he's finished sniffing we invite him to come across to the field with us. I call out to Mom where we're going.

As soon as we cross the street, Homer gallops ahead, checking out gopher holes, rump in the air.

"Clues, clues," Jason mutters as we kick at the stubby grass and pick up candy wrappers and an occasional empty can. Some people are so careless. But we see nothing suspicious.

"We wouldn't," Paloma says. "Iku hasn't been here yet."

"Tonight," Jason says. "I mean, two A.M. tomorrow morning. Then we'll see something, all right." He gives a little excited hop and claps his hands.

"But if we see something . . . if he does come . . . will we really go with him?" That's me asking, wimpy me.

"Of course we will." Jason's nodding and Paloma is, too.

"Of course we will," I say. But I'm thinking: Not in a million years. Earth years or light years either.

Chapter 6

We spend the afternoon making plans. We'll have to sleep in my house or Paloma's, since Jase lives three blocks away from Ocean Field.

"It's all right with me," Mom says when we ask, totally trusting and nice as always. "What are school vacations for but sleepovers?"

Paloma's mom says fine. We can't get through to Jason's, so we ride our bikes over to ask. It's okay for him, too, after he tells his mom five hundred times that he's feeling great, wonderful, healthy, and totally well. Also, Crazy Daisy is having three of her

40

friends to their house, so his mom is pretty relieved not to have Jase. And Jase is super relieved not to have to be there.

"I don't want you catching cold again," his mom says, putting a clean cover on his pillow. "But I guess it's okay since you'll be inside." None of us look at her. Our moms are all so innocent.

We go back to Ocean Field to check our hiding place. We'll be here, in our quarters in the shelter, at one o'clock, just in case there's a difference in *their* time difference. It could be complicated.

"I'm going to bring my camera," Jason says. "It takes pictures in the dark with no flash. Hey! Maybe I'll get the first-ever photograph inside a wormhole."

Paloma nods, "Great idea. And I'll bring my whistle. A security measure."

"Sure," I say. "Blow it and the space police will come."

Paloma giggles.

In the stubby grass of Ocean Field we find the right place to put down the guiding

rocks. I've brought the Iku pictures and I point to Surfers' Clock and then to the lighthouse. "If we take a reading and draw a line from here to here, the rocks should go where the lines meet."

Jason looks puzzled.

"Imaginary lines," Paloma tells him.

We make two piles of twigs and shells where tonight we'll place the rocks. It's like a game and I'm enjoying it. We've played games over here in Ocean Field for as long as I can remember. This seems no different. Because tonight and two A.M. tomorrow morning are not here yet and may never be.

We crouch behind the shelter wall to make sure we'll have a good sighting. Jason thinks we should bring Homer.

"I bet he won't come," Paloma says.

"I could leash him," I say. "He hates his leash, but—"

Paloma interrupts. "We should bring him, just in case."

"In case of what?" I ask, but Paloma only shrugs.

Chapter 7

It's a true fact that waiting for something good—or something bad—is hard! We sit on one of the long green benches on the bluff, staring down at the ocean. Surfers skitter on the big waves. Sailboats bounce in the wind.

Way below us, the people on the amusement pier cluster, small as bees. Sometimes the wind brings happy screams from the roller coaster. The Ferris wheel turns and turns, no bigger than the wheel in a hamster cage.

"Why do you think Iku chose us?" Paloma asks.

"He didn't. We chose him." Jason pulls the newspaper ad out of his pocket. It's folded small as a postage stamp. When he opens it, the headline WANNA BUY AN ALIEN? screams at us in big black letters.

"I guess, up on Cham, they figure anyone who answers this ad is interested in space," I say, and then I add, "Hey, maybe there'll be other kids up there."

"What do you mean?" Paloma is tweaking her hair. "You mean other kids answered the ad and stayed?"

"We're not hanging around on Cham more than three hours," Jase says. "Iku said we'll be back before we're missed. I don't want to stay."

We sit in silence, thinking this over.

"Let's ask him before we get in his ship," Jason suggests.

We keep tilting our heads back to check the sky. There's nothing up there but blueness and a few wispy clouds and sea birds and now and then a plane that looks no big-

ger than my hand. No bigger than Iku's hand.

We watch Surfers' Clock. I'm thinking of the things I've read about space quakes, and exploding stars. What if we collide with one of those?

At four o'clock the bird we call Pelican Pete comes swooping down to sit on the railing. At the same time, old Melinda May shuffles along the path, her shopping cart rattling in front of her. She starts throwing the fish she's brought in her chewed-up red bucket one by one into Pelican Pete's bill. At five after four, the fish have been swallowed and Pelican Pete flippity-flops away. Melinda May rattles on. Same as every other day.

It's getting cold. The evening wind is coming up. I shiver. I'm jumpy and jittery all of a sudden. Maybe I'm getting sick. Maybe I picked up Jase's flu. Maybe I'll miss out on tonight. Relief swamps me and I slump down in the bench. Man, I wouldn't actually be too unhappy if I missed tonight.

Looking out at the sea, at the surfers coming in, the sailboats tacking for Bates Harbor, tonight is beginning to seem too close.

It's five now by Surfers' Clock. We go home.

We play Myst on Dad's computer, exploring its strange worlds. But playing makes me nervous because we'll soon be in a real strange world ourselves. If Iku comes . . . if we go with him . . . None of us seems really interested in the game and pretty soon we give up.

Mom brings chicken from Pick 'n' Lick, but we're not hungry.

"Oh, my," she says. "Is everybody feeling okay? What about the O'Brien Potatoes? Paloma? They're your favorites."

"No thanks, Mrs. Jackson," Paloma says.

We go in my room, listen to the Beatles, read my Archie comics, fight halfheartedly over the new one. We go out to visit the turtles, who have finished with the snails and are happy to see us bring them cantaloupe slices for dessert. We offer Homer some cantaloupe, which he usually likes, but he's too full of leftover Pick 'n' Lick chicken and turns up his nose.

Back in my room we squint through the blind slats at Ocean Field. Nothing's happening. We check the sky. Only the moon and a few million stars half hidden in the clouds.

At eight-thirty we get in our sleeping bags on the floor of the den and watch my tape of *Jurassic Park*. Homer's stretched out warm and long between me and Paloma. In the kitchen Mom and Dad are on their forty-fourth championship game of Scrabble.

We check out our supplies, which we've hidden in our sleeping bags. Jase has his camera, his flashlight, his two dictionaries, English/Spanish and English/Italian.

"How come?" I ask.

"Well, who knows what they speak on Cham. On the tape Iku didn't sound very

American to me. Besides, they're paperback and they'll fit in my pockets."

Paloma has her "just-in-case" whistle and the little box of See's candy she got for Christmas and has been resisting ever since.

"For Iku," she says. "For—you know—for giving us the ride and the adventure. I wonder if they have See's candy on Cham?"

"They don't in New York," Jase says, "My Aunt Gloria always takes a trillion boxes back with her. Do you think they have dogs there?"

"What about turtles?" Paloma asks. "It's going to be so cool finding out all this stuff."

I'm trying to decide if he and Paloma are as okay about this as they sound. Well, maybe I sound all right, too. What's keeping me going is that *(a)* this whole thing still might be a put-on. Iku won't come and we'll feel like a bunch of doofuses. I might be a happy doofus. Or *(b)* if he does come, we'll be hidden, and we won't have to go. If the other two go and I don't, will they think I'm super chicken? For sure—if they go, I'll have to go. There's no way out of that. Unless I faint. I might. No kidding.

On the TV Tyrannosaurus rex is on the rampage. I hardly notice.

I wish it was morning and I'd wake up and I'd still be here, safe in my sleeping bag. I wish that more than anything.

Chapter 8

We'd thought about leaving the red rocks outside in the yard in the paper bag. But suppose it rained? Or somebody stole them?

"Or suppose there was a mistake and they guided Iku into your yard?" Jason asked.

"Your parents would have conniptions," Paloma said. "My mom, too!"

So in the end we left them in the bag, put the bag in my blue backpack, wrapped the whole thing in a big plastic sheet, and hid it in the toolshed at the bottom of our yard.

"There should be asbestos around it," Jason said.

But who has asbestos?

By eleven the dinosaurs on TV are under control again.

Mom and Dad come in and turn off the set and tell us they're going to bed and they don't want to hear any more talking. Dad locks the French doors and hides the key where he always hides it, under the Chinese bowl on the coffee table.

It's quiet outside.

Now and then a car passes.

Paloma's mom's chimes jingle softly in the breeze, sweet as bird songs. We don't talk, but we whisper. We sneak on the TV again with no sound.

It's a quarter to one. I stop the alarm before it goes off and we crawl soundlessly out of our sleeping bags. We're already dressed, except for our jeans and Reeboks. Our jackets are ready. "Just a sec," I say, and I go in the bathroom and leave the note that

I've secretly written for Mom and Dad beside the toothbrushes.

WE HAVE GONE TO THE PLANET CHAM
WITH THE ALIEN IKU.
JASE FOUND HIM AT 1-800-AN-ALIEN.

I'm leaving the note, just in case. As Paloma said about bringing Homer. Just in case of what? I don't answer myself.

"Ready?" Paloma asks when I go back in the living room.

I nod.

She unlocks the French doors.

"Come on, Homer," I whisper. "Let's go for a walk."

He's puzzled and sleepy, but he knows that word "walk."

"Be quiet," I tell him. I don't put on his leash yet because he'll fuss, and maybe Mom and Dad will hear and come stop us. Stop us! For a minute I'm tempted to do the fussing myself.

Homer frisks ahead of us across our back yard. Moonlight tips the hairs on his coat with gold. We head for the tool shed, padding silently through the damp grass.

Suddenly I notice something.

I stop.

"Paloma? Did your mom take down her wind chimes?"

"Are you kidding?" she whispers. "My mom never . . . " She tilts her head. "What happened? This is the first time ever in my whole life that I haven't heard those chimes. Maybe she did take them down."

I look up at the sycamore tree. Not a leaf is moving, even though the breeze is cold on my face.

My insides have started to slither around.

"What do you think?" Jason whispers.

"Could be there's wind down here but not up there," I say. But I've never heard of such a thing.

We're passing the turtle pen. The three of them are completely hidden under their shells and they won't some out even when I whisper their names. "Pearl? Coconut? Pineapple?"

No response. My turtles always come out for me. Except when they're hibernating and wouldn't come out for the Great Turtle himself.

"Strawberries!" I whisper. The turtles would sell their shells for a strawberry. But there's no response.

"Something has them scared," Paloma whispers.

"Could be there's a coyote around," Jase suggests.

I don't think so.

And now Homer has run too close to the tool shed. He starts to shake and gets down on his belly, wriggling back toward us. His eyes are wide and wild.

"Put his leash on, quick!" Paloma whispers.

I try to, but he takes off fast, past me, ears back, tail between his legs. Homer is not a tail-between-his-legs kind of dog.

I clench my fists deep in my pockets, "Should we . . . should we give up on this?"

"No way," Jase says fiercely. "This is a once-in-a-lifetime chance. Don't be a wuss, Ben."

"Who's a wuss?" Now I'm fierce, too.

"Sacred promise?" Paloma says and we

stand there in the silent, moonlit garden and place our hands one on top of the other, the way we've done since we were little kids. My hand is in the middle, which is good, because it's shaking. I hope neither of the others notices. This is our promise to stick together whatever happens. All the way to the end.

And then Jase says in a very solemn voice, "May the Force be with us."

I almost add, "Amen."

Chapter 9

We keep going to the tool shed. Moonshine blurs through the dusty window, silvers a giant cobweb.

Paloma lifts the plastic-wrapped bag.

"Is it . . . is it still warm?" I ask.

"Very warm."

"What time is it?" I ask Jason. He has one of those Day-Glo watches where you press a button and the dial lights green. He presses it.

"A quarter of one," he says.

"Can't be. That's the time it was when we came out." Paloma's holding the bundle carefully, her face turned away from it.

Jason looks again, then gives his wrist a shake. "This watch never stops. But it's stopped now. The second hand isn't moving."

"Well, anyway, let's hurry," Paloma says.

I lift a pair of Mom's gardening gloves that are balanced on the edge of the wheelbarrow and pull them on. "Here. Give me the rocks."

"It's okay. Give me the gloves."

I'm mad. Does she think I'm chicken to carry them? "Gimme," I say. "The alien stuff was my gift, not yours." I tug at the plastic.

Paloma and I are bristling at each other, not like friends at all.

"Chill out, will you?" she mutters and shoves the bundle at me. I can feel the heat coming through the backpack, through the plastic, onto my chest. I quickly hold it out at arm's length.

Jason leads the walk across the street to Ocean Field. His camera is a black blob against his chest. Paloma is next, the whistle swaying against the front of her windbreaker. I'm last.

There's not a sound anywhere. It's as if the world is waiting. I look up at the big lighted face of Surfers' Clock. It says a quarter to one. Time has stopped for it, too—for all of us.

I tap Paloma's shoulder. "I think Iku is in the wormhole right now," I say. "I think he went through the mouth at a quarter to one." I feel like dropping the rock bundle and running back home, but I don't. We made the sacred promise.

Here are the twig and shell piles we stacked up. We scrape them away with our feet and I open the backpack and let the rocks tumble out onto the grass.

It's Jase and Paloma who lift them, barehanded, and set them, point up, the way they were in the picture.

Immediately this humming starts and the rocks vibrate. Jase flicks on his flashlight and Paloma hisses, "Put it out. Somebody will see."

In the quick beam of the light I'd seen enough. All those veins in the rocks were

beating and pulsing, like arteries in a heart.

We back away.

"Somebody's activated the rocks," I whisper. "Remote control."

And then we're running, running for the safety of the shelter, and for me it's like running in a nightmare, where your legs are moving but *you're* not. The three of us run through the cloud-shadowed moonlight, through the awful silence. At last we reach the tumbled-down wall of the shelter and cower behind it.

Chapter 10

The full moon is hanging in the fronds of the tattered palm tree.

We have no way of telling time.

Although no one is around, we talk in whispers.

Once we hear a heart-stopping rustling and Paloma blinks on her flashlight. Two raccoons have found a potato chip bag. The light freezes them, and their eyes gleam, big and green, before they turn tail and leave. We can't see the rocks, and though we listen, we hear no sound from them.

I'm wondering where Homer is. I'm

thinking of my safe house, so near and yet so far, across the street there, all in darkness.

"How long do you think we've been here?" Jase asks.

Paloma shivers. "Forever."

"Remember how we were always told not to get into cars with strangers?" I say.

"This is not a car, it's a spaceship," Jase whispers.

"But Iku is definitely a stranger!" Paloma stretches one leg at a time, staying in her crouch.

"I think he has a nice face," Jason says.

"I don't like his nose." Paloma makes a "yuk" sound. "It's a pig nose."

"I think . . . " I begin. But I don't get to say what I think because I see a big round shadow hanging just above the ocean. Where did it come from? It's moving through the sky like a giant bat, its shadow dark as the night itself.

"It's Iku." Jason fumbles the lens cover off his camera and I hear a click and then another. "Oh, man!" He's gasping with excitement. "I just got pictures of a spaceship!"

"Stay down," I hiss.

We watch, disbelieving, as the ship hovers over Ocean Field, then drops silently onto the grass. There's only the hump of it now, a low mound that seems to belong to the field itself.

Jason starts to stand, but I pull him down again. "Wait," I whisper. "Let's see what happens next."

"No wonder we never saw spaceships," Paloma whispers. "We were looking for lights in the sky. There are no lights." She reaches for my hand. Or maybe I reach for hers.

The moon makes it possible to see. We peer over the wall of the shelter.

The hatch at the front of the ship is sliding up now. Steps glide down from the dark space. A small, squat figure appears in the opening. We see him clearly, silver as the

Tin Man, that big round head, the eyes, the big ears. He's motionless on the top step, looking, looking around the field.

If I were standing beside him, it would be exactly like the photograph.

"Why don't we just go over to him?" Jason whispers. He's jittery beside me.

"Wait one more minute," I say.

"But what if he leaves?"

"He—"

And then the voice comes.

"Ben? I resolve that you are there behind the wall. You brought me down with the pointers. No problem to hide, my friend. I am waiting."

Hearing him say my name, knowing that he knows I'm here, makes the hair stand on the back of my neck.

"Oooh, I don't think I like this after all," Paloma whispers.

"Don't be such a baby," Jason says.

"She's not a baby," I whisper. "Leave her alone!"

I pull the hood of my navy blue jacket over my head and hold it so only my eyes are uncovered. Then I snake my head above the wall to look. It weirds me out to think Iku may be staring right at me. Or what if he's coming across the field to grab us?

He's on the bottom step, and as I watch, he puts one foot onto the grass and then stops. It's the way Homer stops when he's pulled too tight on his leash. Something glitters in the moonlight and I squint hard and see a silver wire that snakes behind Iku and into the ship. Does it connect him with the air he needs to breathe? Can he go no farther?

"Ben?" he calls. It's the strangest voice, trying to be soft but sharp as gravel.

I slither back down. "I don't think he can come off those steps," I whisper. "He's linked to the ship. So if we don't want to go after all, we can just stay here and wait him out. Or make a run for home." I try to see how they feel about this, but in the half-dark it's hard to tell. I decide I should speak first.

"I don't want to go," I whisper. "It's too dangerous."

"I don't either." Paloma speaks so quickly that I know she was just waiting for a lead. "Before, it sounded like an adventure. But now . . . well, it's too hairy."

Jason leaps up. "Well, *I* want to go and *you're* not stopping me.

"Jase!" I say, "Remember the sacred promise? We have to stick together. It's two against one. Majority rules. We've seen him. You've got the pictures. That's enough."

"Not for me it isn't," Jase mutters. "Forget the sacred promise!"

I make a grab for his jacket, but he slides his arm out of it and then he's gone, running across Ocean Field.

Chapter 11

Paloma and I peer over the wall. Iku is watching. "Ben," he calls. "I am so cheered that you came."

Of course he'd think Jase is me. I'm his contact, after all.

Jason stops a few yards in front of the spaceship. Iku's speaking again, but I can't hear the words.

Jase takes more pictures.

"Maybe he's just going to do that and come back," Paloma whispers.

Now Jase has let the camera down and he's listening to Iku, who is making these

hand gestures. They're "come aboard" gestures, so gentle, so friendly.

My heart is pounding. I'm numb with fear. I've seen someone act like this before.

Right here. The day we saved Homer. The dog catcher was rounding up dogs on Ocean Field because people had complained. He stood at the back of his van, the rear doors open, and tried to coax the dogs closer with that sweet voice and those nice smiles. "Come, doggie, doggie. Come, fella."

Some went quietly. Others came close, and when they did, the dog catcher snatched them and put them in the back of the van. "He probably has cages," Paloma had said. Homer was heading for that van when we threw our arms around his neck and pulled him back. We held him—just about piled on top of him—till the van took off.

"He's our dog!" we had yelled at the man. And he was, from that very minute.

When I look again, Jase is moving closer to Iku.

"No, Jase, no!" I shout, "Cages!"

Paloma blows her whistle with this ear-deafening blast and the two of us are running through the moonlit dark toward the extraterrestrial with the three-fingered hands and the big searchlight eyes. And it's another nightmare.

Chapter 12

Jason's almost at the bottom of the steps. He stops when he hears my yell and Paloma's whistle and turns toward us.

"Get back! Get back, Jase!" I shout.

But I'm too late.

Iku has stretched out and he's got Jason's arm. He's dragging him up the steps of the spacecraft.

Jason yells, "Hey! Let go of me!"

He may have wanted to go on the spacecraft, but he doesn't like being hauled into it like this.

"Let go of him, you creep!" Paloma screams.

I launch myself at Jason's leg, holding it tight as I try to pull him back down. Paloma has the other leg. We're tugging with all our strength, but Iku's on the other end of Jason and he's stronger than we are, all three of us put together. Superhuman strength. Extraterrestrial strength. We're being jolted up those steps and Iku's winning the terrible tug-o-war.

Paloma and I could let go.

We don't.

We could all three scream.

Two of us do. The third one blows on her whistle, but it doesn't have much blast since she doesn't have much breath anymore.

"Help!" we shout.

"Peep-peep," goes the sorry little whistle.

Iku is at the top of the steps and he has one foot inside the spacecraft. His face isn't nice now. His lips are pulled back in a horrible kind of smile that isn't a smile. Steam is coming out of the holes in his nose— more and more steam, so that there's a cloud of it around his head. Jason starts to cough.

I'm trying desperately to hold on to the railing at the side of the steps, but inch by inch we're going up. "Help! Help!" I call.

It's two o'clock in the morning. Who's going to hear us?

But suddenly something comes hurtling across the field. It's a big yellow dog, growling and snarling. He bounds over us to the top of the steps and he's got Iku's leg in his jaws and Iku is screeching louder than

Paloma can whistle. Steam is coming out of his leg now, blasting up around Homer, and my dog is coughing, too.

Iku lets go of Jason and his three-fingered hand chops at Homer. But Homer grabs that hand in his big drippy jaws and he's biting on it the way he likes to bite on his doggie bone.

Paloma, Jase, and I bump on our bellies down the steps. Then we're running, with

my wonderful, brave, faithful dog bounding along beside us.

We don't stop till we're out in the street, with my house behind us, all four of us panting, two of us with our tongues hanging out. And only one of those two is Homer.

Iku has disappeared. From this safe distance we watch the steps glide up, the hatch

close, and the spaceship rise. It hangs for a minute like an angry thundercloud in the sky.

"He's in orbit," Jason whispers. "Man, we could have been cruising to a galaxy not our own this very minute." There's a sort of ashamed longing in his voice.

"And we might have been looking at it through the bars of those nice cages," I say.

"What?" Paloma asks.

"Nothing." I kneel and put my arms around Homer's neck. "You are the best dog in the world," I tell him. "You were scared and still you came to help us. You are brave, brave, brave." I kiss his soft yellow head.

Paloma turns his face up and kisses him right on his doggie lips, which is something we're not allowed to do. But who cares? "I think there's something that's even stronger than being afraid," she says.

Jason frowns. "What?"

"It's too sappy to say," Paloma tells him.

Maybe she was going to say "love." That *is* too sappy. But it's true.

"Well," Jase says, "I wasn't scared of anything. And with my dictionaries, I could have talked to him."

"I was scared," I say. "Right from the beginning." And I'm thinking that right from the beginning I should have owned up to that. It would have been better.

Surfers' Clock says two-forty-five. So does Jason's watch.

I can't believe it. But I can.

We go single file through our dark, sleepy yard, Homer padding watchfully behind us.

The leaves on the sycamore tree rustle gently.

The turtles lift their heads and nod to us as we pass.

Paloma's mom's wind chimes are singing their wind chime song again.

Iku's gone and our world is back.

We sneak quietly into my house, climb into our sleeping bags, and burrow into their safe softness. I remember the note I left, so I climb out again to get it and crumple it into the wastebasket. When I come back, Jase and Paloma are whispering in the dark.

"We're wondering if we should tell," Paloma says. "Nobody's going to believe us."

"We have to tell," I say. "Maybe Iku's doing this all over California—all over the world, even. Maybe other kids have gone and disappeared."

Paloma pulls the sleeping bag right over her head. Her voice is muffled. "How awful. I can't stand it."

Jase has been droopy, but now he perks up. "We'll go to the FBI. We'll be famous. They'll want us on all the talk shows. Talk shows love extraterrestrials."

"I still wonder if they'll believe us," Paloma says.

"'Course they will. We have all this proof," Jason says.

I'm not so sure.

Chapter 13

It's the next morning and we're feeling pretty discouraged.

We have no proof.

The pictures Iku sent have all changed back to the way they were before. There I am, standing with Jase on the steps of our tree house. No Iku. There I am, climbing the steps, waving at the camera. No Iku. The letter is a blank piece of paper, the kind my cousin Joan makes, and when we listen to the tape, all we hear is our third-grade play.

"I was pretty good," Jase mutters when he

hears his famous one liner: "The horses are ready, sir."

We go back over to Ocean Field. I don't think I'll be able to look at this field again without bad memories, but maybe it will get better. This morning everything's sparkling and sunny. A small class of Tai Chi-ers are working out, gazing peacefully at the sea and the sky, where last night a spaceship hung, dark and menacing.

The pointers have gone. There are just two round circles of scorched grass, grape-fruit-size, where last night the red veined rocks pulsed and hummed.

Jason's jacket is lying where I dropped it. My backpack, too, and Mom's gloves.

"I can't believe it ever happened," Paloma says.

Who will? Nobody.

Back in my room we sit on my bed eating See's candies and staring at our lost evidence. The Beatles are singing "Twist and Shout," which we would normally find very cheerful. But we're not cheerful today.

"Don't forget. We still have the photographs I took," Jase says. "*The National Enquirer* is going to pay a fortune for those."

We sit at the kitchen table, quiet over our breakfast pancakes.

"I bet you guys are exhausted," Mom says. "I bet you talked all night."

We nod and half smile. If she only knew! And she will.

First we have to get Jase's pictures.

We ride our bikes to the photo shop and pay extra to get one-hour developing.

"Be careful of that film," Jase says. "Those are valuable pictures."

We hang around, waiting.

When the guy gives them back, he smirks at Jason and says, "Yeah. Very valuable."

I think I knew all the time that the pictures would be blank.

The guy leans across the counter. "Next time, remember to take off the lens cap, dude."

"I took it off," Jase says and we chorus: "He took it off!"

So we have nothing.

But we have to tell anyway.

We call a serious parents' meeting. The last time we called one was when we went to the Cineplex to see *Blood of the Vampire*, which none of us had permission to see. We were supposed to be in after-school craft class. Unfortunately, Mrs. Chalmers, our English teacher, was at the movie and saw us. She's a friend of Paloma's mom's, so we knew she'd blab and we decided we should tell first.

And then Mrs. Chalmers never did blab, which shows how you can misjudge people—especially English teachers.

"We should have known she'd be cool if she went to *Blood of the Vampire* in the first place," Paloma had said. But by then we'd had our meeting and confessed.

This meeting is different. Our parents know it's something crucial and Jase's parents even give up their weekly bowling night to come.

We meet at Paloma's house. Her mom is an artist so all the walls are hung with pretty paintings of sunflowers and marigolds and tulips. It's very soothing in that room filled with flowers, but we're not soothed.

I have been chosen to tell.

Our parents listen carefully and don't interrupt except for a few gasps and mutters and head shakings.

At the end they look at each other. Then they all begin talking at once.

"Over in that dark field, alone, the three of you in the middle of the night. There could have been all kinds of weird people there!" (Doesn't my mom realize there *were?*)

"And, Jason, you just getting over a cold!" His mom leans across to feel his forehead.

"You say this space vehicle came down? And you saw a spaceman?" his dad asks.

They're our parents and they love us. But we can tell this story is hard for them to digest.

They ask Jason if he's brought the ad. He hasn't, but his mom remembers him answering it and all the excitement. I wouldn't be surprised if it's blank, too, when we look at it again.

The talk goes back and forth.

They say they are disappointed in us. They say they always thought they could trust us. They seem to have forgotten about *Blood of the Vampire.*

There are long pauses when they fidget and tap their fingers on the arms of their chairs and look anxiously at each other and at us.

My dad says, "It was good, though, that you decided to tell us. We know you didn't have to."

"And we're glad you had enough sense not to go with that Iku person, whoever he was." That's Jason's dad and Jase gives a little guilty shrug.

They believe us.

But only sort of.

They agree, though, that the police have to be told.

"Whether the guy came from space or not, he seems to be luring kids and he has to be stopped," my dad says.

"You don't think it was someone in school playing an elaborate trick on you?" Paloma's mom asks.

Paloma shakes her head. "No, Mom. No, no, no."

So the next morning they troop the three of us down to the police station. The officers are polite and friendly and take lots of notes. We make statements and sign them. They say they'll definitely investigate. Con merchants who get forty bucks a pop from kids are lower than snakes. On the way out, passing the front desk, I think I hear one officer say to another: "Hey, when I was a kid, it was cops and robbers."

So what it comes down to is that nobody really believes. As Paloma says, nobody ever believes about extraterrestrials. That's a true fact.

But we know.

We know we weren't playing cops and robbers.

We know we didn't imagine any of it.

And we know there should be a warning.

So this is it:

ATTENTION!!

IF YOU ARE READING OUR STORY, BE ADVISED. IF SOMEONE OFFERS YOU AN ALIEN FOR SALE, BEWARE. THERE COULD BE VERY SERIOUS CONSEQUENCES.

YOU HAVE BEEN WARNED!!!

signed,

Ben

JASON

Paloma

(Homer)